Fair Helen's Midnight

by

D.L. John

Illustrated by Kirnan John

DORRANCE
PUBLISHING CO
EST. 1920
PITTSBURGH, PENNSYLVANIA 15238

Dorrance Publishing Co
585 Alpha Drive
Suite 103
Pittsburgh, PA 15238
Visit our website at *www.dorrancebookstore.com*

ISBN: 978-1-6491-3769-2
eISBN: 978-1-6491-3957-3

Fair Helen's Midnight

Escapism for this moment

Fair Helen St. Lucie
granted herself a day
to rediscover her depth.

With all the disturbances
and despondency,
she needed a walk.

From her soils within,
Helen formed an image
for a journey at dawn.

She stretched
like the bamboo,
felt some grace
and started at a slow pace.

Helen's hibiscuses
tailored a beautiful
petal skirt
that brightened
as she walked
through the rising sun.

She marveled as the
colours danced in the
fresh winds of the dewy
morning,
a welcoming cool.

Her regal Amazona -
versicolor and other
feathered friends
granted her some of their
plumage for her bosom.

Just then Sir Whiptail
came into sight.

"Why not," she thought,
"scuttle with him
and Mister Racer."

She felt increased agility,
moving so freely.

She checked her scars
from plantations
and forts.

Helen felt no remorse,
but forgiveness
and thankfulness,
as these spots had
transformed with time.

"After all, my history
did shape me a tad!"
she said with a shrug
and a chuckle.

Fair Helen walked
through her towns
and villages with a bit
of Madras wrapped
around her head.

With a hint of distress
for some of her
traditions and art,
like the diligent
moulding hands of the
coal pot maker
and basket weaver being
sparingly seen about,
she kept hope.

Hope that the old
traditions will reform
and perhaps,
create a new.

She felt the fierceness
and beauty bubbling
more within herself,
just as her
sulphur springs.

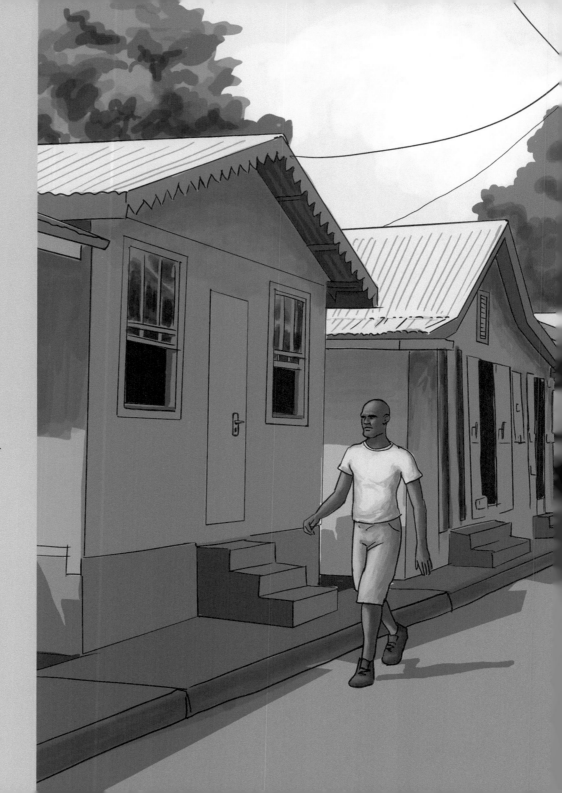

As dusk settled in,
she strolled and
watched peacefully
as her fishermen
repaired their nets.

She picked up a few shells
and threaded them
around her ankle.

Feeling content
as the sun had set,
she gave back the
petals and plumage,
threw some seeds
to set her mind at ease,
and breezed over
to her peaks.

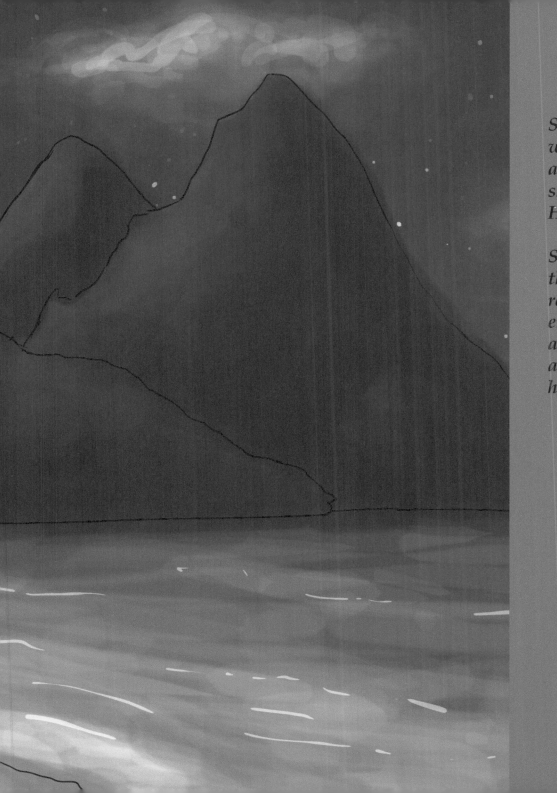

She saw dear Lune
was full,
and as a tribute to herself,
she decided to dance
Helen's Midnight.

She borrowed
the night's gems
reflected in her waters,
embellished herself
and danced
among her peaks into
her lovely warm waters.

Fair Helen's dreams
that night were filled
with serenity
for all discovered.

She vowed to take
shape once again
and walk to see what
future discoveries
that time would trail out
within her.

Colour Your Tranquil

CPSIA information can be obtained
at www.ICGtesting.com
Printed in the USA
LVHW071157260621
691169LV00004B/14